GLOBAL LEGENDS AND LORE

Vampires and Werewolves Around the World

THE MAKING OF A MONSTER

& WEREWOLVES

Ancient Werewolves and Vampires:
The Roots of the Teeth

Dracula and Beyond: Famous Vampires &
Werewolves in Literature and Film

Fighting the Fangs: A Guide to Vampires and
Werewolves

Howling at the Moon: Vampires & Werewolves in
the New World

Pop Monsters: The Modern-Day Craze for
Vampires and Werewolves

The Psychology of Our Dark Side: Humans' Love
Affair with Vampires & Werewolves

The Science of the Beast:
The Facts Behind the Fangs

Transylvania and Beyond: Vampires &
Werewolves in Old Europe

Global Legends and Lore: Vampires and
Werewolves Around the World

GLOBAL LEGENDS AND LORE

Vampires and Werewolves Around the World

by Adelaide Bennett

Mason Crest Publishers

MASON CREST PUBLISHERS INC.
370 Reed Road
Broomall, Pennsylvania 19008
(866)MCP-BOOK (toll free)
www.masoncrest.com

First Printing
9 8 7 6 5 4 3 2 1

ISBN (series) 978-1-4222-1801-3
Paperback ISBN (series) 978-1-4222-1954-6

Library of Congress Cataloging-in-Publication Data

Bennett, Adelaide.
 Global legends and lore : vampires and werewolves around the world / by Adelaide Bennett.
     p. cm.
 Includes bibliographical references (p.   ) and index.
 ISBN 978-1-4222-1810-5 (hardcover)   ISBN 978-1-4222-1963-8 (pbk.)
 1. Vampires. 2. Werewolves. I. Title.
 GR830.V3B47 2011
 398.21—dc22
                                    2010025778

Produced by Harding House Publishing Service, Inc.
www.hardinghousepages.com
Interior design by MK Bassett-Harvey.
Cover design by Torque Advertising + Design.
Printed in the USA by Bang Printing.

CONTENTS

1. Blood: Our Fascination with Life and Death 7

2. The Blood-Thirsty Monsters of Europe 15

3. Asia's Blood-Drinking Creatures 29

4. Africa's Living Dead 41

5. Australian Blood Suckers 47

6. The Americas' Bloody Beasts 51

Words You May Not Know 60

Find Out More on the Internet 61

Further Reading 61

Bibliography 62

Index 63

About the Author 64

Picture Credits 64

chapter 1
BLOOD: OUR FASCINATION WITH LIFE AND DEATH

Down through the ages, humans have always been fascinated with blood. It is the magic liquid within our bodies that keeps us alive. Even today, with all our scientific knowledge of red and white blood cells, platelets, and antibodies, blood remains mysterious and amazing.

Blood, from the very beginning of our history, has represented human life. Women bleed when their bodies become capable of creating new life. Newborns come into the world through blood. Generation after generation, we pass our blood on into the future through our children and their children. Blood flows through our veins, fills our bodies, fuels our hearts, and sustains our existence. If we lose enough of it, we die, and so blood not only symbolizes life; it also means death. And to give blood to another can mean life.

Ancient humans understood this connection between blood and life and death. In Homer's *Odyssey*, the ancient Greek epic, Odysseus pours blood into a lifeless body so that he can talk with it. In Australia, the Aborigines believed that blood was the strength of life that feeds and nourishes the soul. The ancient Aztec people believed that by drinking another's blood, you could be strengthened with that person's soul, which was seen as an honor.

In the ancient world, blood's connection to women, to menstruation, and to childbirth was both honored and feared. The Egyptian goddess Sekhmet (who looked like a woman with a lion's head) was the goddess of menstruation. She was called the Scarlet Lady—but she was also a goddess of war, known as the One Before Whom Evil Trembles and the Lady of the Slaughter. She was known for her thirst for blood, a thirst that could become dangerous and out of control. Ancient people often saw women as powerful and creative—and also powerful and destructive.

The human obsession with blood also reveals itself in the many ancient cultures that practiced blood sacrifice. The Old Testament Jews conducted blood sacrifices with animals, but on one occasion, the patriarch

The Goddess Sekhmet was a woman with a lion's head, a combination that made her both fierce and proud.

Abraham was ready to sacrifice his son to God, but an angel stopped him in the nick of time.

Abraham was willing to spill even his son's blood in an offering to God, if an angel had not stopped him. Meanwhile, on the other side of the world, the Aztecs and the Mayans laid down human lives for their gods. They believed that divine fire flowed from a person's heart through his blood and into his body—and to spill that blood and take the heart was to release the gods' fire.

Such beliefs may seem primitive and repulsive to us, but we are not so different from our ancestors as we might think. Many modern-day Christians regularly enact a blood ritual as part of their worship. In the New Testament, Christ made the connection between blood, life, and the soul when he ate his last meal with his friends and symbolically offered his blood to them, saying, "This is my blood which shall be given up for you." Christianity's central ritual, Holy Eucharist (or Communion), memorializes and repeats again and again Christ's final meal of metaphorical blood and flesh. Some Christians believe it is not a metaphor, but the actual blood and flesh of Jesus that Christians consume at the communion table.

The human fascination with blood shows up in story after story, in many shapes and forms. In the myth of the Holy Grail, for example, the grail is also called "Sangreal," meaning "royal blood." The magical cup is said to have been the one Christ used at the Last Supper when he shared his blood symbolically with his friends, and then was used again at the Cross to catch his actual blood as he died. The Grail represents many things in different stories, but they all have to do with the mysterious life force that fills our bodies, with fertility and potency, with hope and life, with death and resurrection—all connected back again to blood.

Since the earliest humans huddled around a fire, blood has been used to honor the gods, span the gap

BLOOD AND PERSONALITY

The word blood is used in many figures of speech in the English language, indicating the ways we connect blood with our identities. For instance, we talk about people who belong to the elite as being "blue-blooded" (though of course their blood isn't really blue). Thin-blooded means someone gets cold easily. Hot-blooded indicates that a person has a quick temper, while cold-blooded means a person is cruel and unfeeling. Warm-blooded, on the other hand, means that someone is full of vitality, as does red-blooded. Red-blooded can also mean that a person is full of patriotism. Bad blood has to do with relationship problems between groups of people. If you have "blood on your hands," you are guilty of a crime, and something that is "blood-curdling" is terrifying.

between life and death, and nourish both the body and the spirit. Vampire and werewolf stories—creatures who must drink human blood in order to live—are just one more variation on this ancient theme. Blood is what allowed Count Dracula—and Anne Rice's Lestat and many other fictional vampires—to live for centuries.

For the vampire and the werewolf, blood is both life and death. In the fiction of the past two centuries, the vampire's act of consuming another's blood has been portrayed as both evil and as a source of ecstasy and transformation, for both the victim and the vampire.

This portrayal of the vampire brings to life our feelings about death. Death is the ultimate darkness, the ultimate mystery. It both fascinates and terrifies us. When we look at it, we see two faces: one is forbidding and evil, while the other offers us the hope and joy of new life, the ultimate transformation to a higher level of being. We have no way of knowing for sure which face is real. Perhaps they both are.

Does blood represent the beginning of life—or its end? Does it offer terror—or hope? Is a bleeding woman a symbol of fertility and new life—or a threatening figure of endless thirst and emptiness? Through the centuries and around the world, humans have put flesh on these questions with stories of conflicted creatures of the night, vampires and werewolves who contain within their fearsome shapes the duality of life and death.

chapter 2
THE BLOOD-THIRSTY MONSTERS OF EUROPE

When we think of European blood-drinkers, our first thoughts are probably of Dracula, the classic bat-caped, fang-toothed, debonair vampire of Eastern Europe's gloomy castles. But Europe has many other less famous monsters that also embody the human fascination with blood.

The British Isles

The Celtic world is full of these creatures. The Baobban Sith (pronounced "bahvan shee," which means "spirit woman") are the female vampires of Ireland that look like beautiful young women dressed in green gowns. Their long skirts hide their cloven hooves, though sometimes, they can also appear as crows or ravens. In their human form, they lure young men to dance with them, but when the dance is over, they leave behind great bloody wounds on the men's necks and shoulders. Luckily, horses terrify them and drive them away.

Hungry Grass: Vampire Earth?

In Ireland, a place where someone died of starvation is called "Fear Gortagh," which means "hungry grass." The hunger is thought to linger there, and if a living person spends too much time in that spot, the hunger can suck up their vital energy.

The Irish also believed in terrible tiny vampires, blood-drinking fairies. These were sometimes known as Dreach-Fhoula (which is pronounced "drocola" and means "bad or tainted blood"). The word has come to be used for blood feuds, but scholars believe it has a deeper, darker meaning. Some have suggested that the word may have inspired Bram Stoker, author of *Dracula*, as much as Transylvania's Vlad Dracula did.

Across the Irish Sea, the Green Woman haunted Scotland. Her upper body was that of a beautiful woman, but her lower body

Not all fairies were pretty and sweet. Some were tiny, evil bloodsuckers!

Irish spirit women could appear as beautiful women (with goat feet hidden beneath their long gowns) or as shape-shifting crow women.

was a goat's. Her skin was gray, and her long golden hair fell over her shoulders. Like the spirit women of Ireland, she did her best to hide her goatish legs beneath a green gown. Although she was prone to drinking the blood of young men, she was often kind to children and elderly folk, and she would sometime herd a farmer's cows for him. In gratitude, people made her offerings of milk.

Why Are There No Werewolves in the British Isles?

All the wolves were killed in the British Isles centuries ago, when the Anglo Saxons still ruled the islands, which perhaps explains why there are so few werewolf stories. Instead, witches are sometimes said to take the shape of cats or huge black dogs, running across the moors in animal form by night, old ladies by day.

Kirghiz avec un aigle royal

England's Redcaps, meanwhile, were totally evil creatures drawn to places where human blood had been spilled. They not only drank the blood, but soaked in it (hence the color of their caps). Redcaps could be resisted by reciting the Bible or by brandishing a cross in their faces. They would then flee in terror, leaving behind one of their teeth, running as fast as their magic iron boots would carry them.

Russia

Several kinds of blood-sucking creatures infested the deep forests of Russia. Failing to conform to the Christian faith in Russia put a person at risk of becoming a vampire. One of the undead, a "heretic," for instance, was a vampire who had ended his human life outside the faith, after selling his soul to the devil. Sometimes, sorcerers would create these creatures by reanimating dead bodies, which would then feed on the blood of their relatives. Looking into the eyes of one of these creatures would cause a slow and withering death.

The Mjertovjec were werewolf-vampires with purple faces, creatures that haunted the darkness from midnight until the cock crowed the third time in the morning. These were actually the ghosts of werewolves and sorcerers—or sometimes, merely the ghost of someone who had cursed his own father during a church service. Sprinkling poppy seeds along the road that led from his tomb to his former house could destroy this monster. A nail through the coffin would usually do the trick as well.

The Upierczi were creatures who become vampires after a suicide, a violent death, or practicing witchcraft during their lifetime. Their breath was so hot that it dried the dew on the grass and could even cause droughts. They could be destroyed by drowning them in freshwater (a river or a lake, but not the ocean). Driving a nail through their bodies would sometimes work as well, but you needed to be careful to drive the nail in with a single blow. If you hit the nail more than once, the body would revive and rise up to suck your blood.

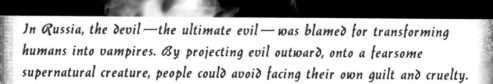

In Russia, the devil —the ultimate evil — was blamed for transforming humans into vampires. By projecting evil outward, onto a fearsome supernatural creature, people could avoid facing their own guilt and cruelty.

Another kind of vampire, the Wampir, looked exactly like normal humans—except they had stingers beneath their tongues, useful for stunning their victims before sucking their blood. Unlike most blood-sucking creatures, the Wampir were active by daylight, from noon until midnight. The only way to get rid of these creatures was to burn them, but even then, you had to be careful. When flames consumed a Wampir's body, it would burst, and hundreds of maggots, rats, and insects would spill out of it. Each one of these had to be carefully tracked down and destroyed; if one were to get away, the Wampir's spirit would escape as well, and it would later return to seek revenge.

Meanwhile, the Wurdulac is Russia's classic werewolf-vampire, a tragic creature condemned to feast only on the people it loved in life. As a result, entire families could be transformed into Wurdulacs. Once a Wurdulac has eaten through his entire family, he must form new relationships, because only the blood of someone he loves can nourish him. In some stories, the Wurdulac starves to death rather than make new friends. By destroying himself, he ends the chain of death.

Scandinavia

Werewolves and were-bear were thought to roam the cold, northern lands of the Scandinavian countries. In Norway, this story was told:

In a hamlet in the midst of a forest, there dwelt a cottager named Lasse, and his wife. One day he went out in the forest to fell a tree, but had forgot to cross himself and say his paternoster [the Lord's Prayer], so that some troll or wolf-witch obtained power over him and transformed him into a wolf. His wife mourned him for many years, but, one Christmas Eve, there came a beggar-woman, very poor and ragged, to the door, and the good woman of the house took her in, fed her well, and entreated her kindly. At her departure the beggar-woman said that the wife would probably see her husband again, as he was not dead, but was wandering in the forest as a wolf. Towards nightfall, the wife went to her pantry to place in it a piece of meat for the morrow, when, on turning to go out, she perceived a wolf standing before her, raising itself with its paws on the pantry steps, regarding her with sorrowful and hungry looks. Seeing this she exclaimed, "If I were sure that thou wert my own Lasse, I would give thee a bit of meat." At that instant the wolf-skin fell off, and her husband stood before her in the clothes he wore on the unlucky morning when she had last beheld him.

People could also be born as were-creatures. A woman who wanted to avoid pain during childbirth could do so by crawling through the amniotic sack of a foal at midnight. She would then be able to give birth painlessly—but her sons would all be werewolves and her daughters would be were-mares. The werewolves would be able to be recognized while in their human

In lands where wolves howled in the night, werewolves haunted human nightmares. In lands where there were no wolves, however, stories grew of other creatures: were-bears, were-cats, or even were-mares.

forms by the way their eyebrows met above their noses. They could be freed from their curse if another person recognized their identity and spoke it out loud.

An example of this was told in a story from Denmark:

A man, who from his childhood had been a were-wolf, when returning one night with his wife from a merrymaking, observed that the hour was at hand when the evil usually came upon him; giving therefore the reins to his wife, he descended from the vehicle, saying to her, "If anything comes to thee, only strike at it with thine apron." He then withdrew, but immediately after, the woman, as she was sitting in the vehicle, was attacked by a were-wolf. She did as the man had enjoined her, and struck it with her apron, from which it rived a portion, and then ran away. After some time the man returned, holding in his mouth the rent portion of his wife's apron, on seeing which, she cried out in terror, "Good Lord, man, why, thou art a were-wolf!"

"Thank thee, wife," said he, "now I am free." And from that time he was no more afflicted.

Many Scandinavians blamed trolls for turning people into werewolves, but they also blamed their enemies, including the Lapps and the Russians. During times of war with Russia, if the land was overrun with an unusual number of wolves, rumors would fly that the Russians had transformed their

Ancient European legends tell tales of people who were half human, half wolf.

prisoners into wolves and sent them home to infest their homeland.

Other forms of witchcraft could also transform a person into a bloodthirsty creature. In one village, for example, many people were said to have a girdle (a belt) made of human skin, which they could wear to change themselves into werewolves whenever the fancy took them. Obviously, this was the sort of thing you would want to keep away from little children, but one day, a father carelessly left it lying out where his young son found it and buckled it on. The little boy immediately turned into something that looked like a ball of straw and began rolling around the floor. His father grabbed him and unbuckled the girdle before his son could do any harm. As soon as he was back in his human skin, the little boy said he had been so hungry he'd been ready to tear to pieces and devour anything that got in his way.

Eastern Europe

Of course, the classic vampire is the most familiar creature of Eastern Europe—but the Dracula we know and love today was not actually based on the folklore of this region so much as it was the creation of an Englishman's imagination. And there are other, lesser-known monsters in the dark forests of Transylvania and beyond.

In Poland, for example, the Luderc appears as a burning shaft of light that flies through the night sky. It enters a house through the chimney, where it takes on the appearance of a dead marriage partner and crawls in bed with its victim. The man or woman will be pale and weak in the morning, with no energy. The only way to rid yourself

Stay Away from Seven Sisters

In some Scandinavian regions, people believed that if a family had seven daughters, one of them had to be a werewolf. As a result, young men were slow to court one of seven sisters.

In the folklore of the Scandinavian countries, trolls, were-creatures, and vampires are often connected.

of a Luderc, once one has attached itself to you, is to exorcise them with magic.

The Nora was another vampire creature, a tiny bald imp that ran on all fours. It would drink the blood from the breasts of immoral women, making them swell painfully. The remedy for this ailment was to cover the affected breasts with garlic, which would prevent the Nora from attacking again.

The Human Heritage of Blood

These stories speak of sorrow and sin, guilt and terror, but they all focus on blood as a common ingredient. The bloodthirsty creatures that haunted Europe were the stuff of nightmares—and yet for those of us with an European heritage, these stories probably make a peculiar kind of dark sense. Thousands of miles to the east, however, in Asia, different stories were being told. The creatures in these tales may seem strange (depending on our ethnic backgrounds), and yet in some ways, they are hauntingly the same.

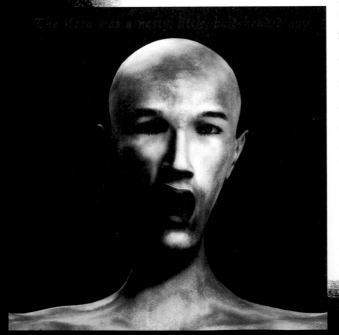

The Nora was a nasty little bald-headed imp.

27

chapter 3
ASIA'S BLOOD-DRINKING SPIRITS

Asia is an enormous continent, and its monsters are many and varied. From the island of Japan to the islands in the Pacific to the mountains of Tibet, blood-thirsty creatures roam the nights, terrifying beasts with pale, cold skin and terrible hungers.

Japan

The Japanese Gaki are wailing corpses that thirst for blood. In their own form, they look like pale-skinned, hollow-eyed humans, but they can shape shift into both animals and other humans, thus hiding their true nature. If you touch the hand of a Gaki, however, when it is posing as a living human, its skin will feel like cold, damp earth.

The Hannya, meanwhile, was once a beautiful woman who became insane. A demon possessed her, changing her into a hideous creature that drank blood and ate children.

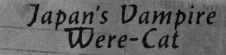

Japan's Vampire Were-Cat

One of the most insidious of Japan's monsters was a shape-shifting vampire cat that sucked the lifeblood from its victim, then buried the body and took the victim's shape as its own. It would go on next to prey upon the victim's unsuspecting loved ones.

She is a spiritual daughter of the Egyptian goddess Sekhmet, a hungry woman desperate for blood.

Particularly nasty creatures called Kappa sometimes inhabit Japan's streams and lakes. These horrifying beings look like terrible green-skinned children. They drag horses and cows into their watery homes, where they suck the blood from the animals' anuses. As if that weren't bad enough, they can leave the water when they want to rape women or steal people's livers, which they consume as a delicacy.

The Kasha are a quite different creature, ghouls with a voracious appetite for corpses and blood. Because of the Japanese cremation custom, these creatures must steal a corpse before it can be burned; they would often

Japanese folklore is full of fierce demons and terrifying creatures.

make off with the body, coffin and all, and so guards were once placed over the dead to make noise during the night, scaring away the Kasha.

China

Across the sea on Asia's mainland, other terrifying creatures haunted the night, seeking blood. The Ch'iang Shih, for example, were demons that could inhabit any dead body. They could even create a new being from a few broken bones and scraps of rotted flesh. The Ch'iang Shih's red eyes glowed in the dark, their damp, moldy

odor warning travelers they were near. Their long fingernails were as sharp as vulture's talons, their teeth were long and serrated like a knife, and hair the color of pale green mold grew on their bodies. Occasionally, you might see one with pink hair instead of green. These terrible beasts would leap out of graves and attack travelers in the dark; if the Ch'iang Shih survived long enough to mature, they learned to fly, making them even more dangerous. If they snatched an unwary traveler along a dark road, they would first suck out his blood. When he was dead and white, they would go on to their second course and devour his bloodless flesh. These creatures could also transform themselves into wolves—and like their cousins to the West, they were allergic to garlic.

The Jiangshi—also known as the "blood-sucking ghost" or a "hopping corpse"—is the classic Chinese vampire, popular in many horror movies. It could be put back to sleep by placing on its forehead a spell written on a piece of paper.

The Philippines

On the Philippine Islands, the Aswang walks as a beautiful maiden by day—and flies as a fearsome fiend by night. She lives a normal life during the sunlit hours, and her friends and family may never know her true nature. Each night, however, small dark owls lead her to a victim's house. She perches on the roof and inserts her long, pointed, tubular tongue like a terrible straw down into the bedroom below, where she pierces the skin of her sleeping victim and sucks out the blood. On the nights she drinks too much, the next day, she will look swollen; her friends may even think she is pregnant. In her human form, she occasionally will be unable to resist taking a lick of a person's shadow. If she does, the person will die soon afterward.

In some regions of the Philippines, however, the Aswang takes another form. In this case, it can be either male or female, and again, by day, it appears to be a normal human. At night, however, its top half separates from its lower half; the top half then grows wings and flies off to seek human blood. Its favorite delicacy is said to be the unborn babies it snatches from their mothers' wombs. If you find its lower half and cover it with salt, the two parts of its body cannot be rejoined, and it will die.

The Wrathful Deities

Also known as the fifty-eight blood-drinking deities, these vampires represent various aspects of a dead person's personality. Since all of us have selfish urges and evil tendencies, during the days after we die, say the Thai, these "wrathful deities," the dark parts of our souls, walk the spirit world.

Kirghiz avec un aigle

Yet another version of Aswang tells of a particular young girl who was the most beautiful woman on her island. When she was sixteen years old, she married a strong young man. As soon as they were married, he began to grow weak and thin, and after a year of marriage, he withered away and died. She married another strong young man soon after, and he suffered the same fate as her first husband. The same thing happened with her third husband. She then married a fourth husband, but he was understandably nervous about his new wife. He went to bed with a knife under his pillow and pretended to fall asleep. Before long, he felt something prick his neck, and he struck out with his knife. It was too dark for him to see the creature he stabbed, but he heard a screech and the sound of flapping wings. In the morning, he found his wife lying dead outside their cottage, a knife wound in her chest.

Thailand

The ancient land of Thailand swarms with spirits. The Krassy, for example, are old women who fly at night, seeking babies' blood. If they can't find their preferred meal, they'll dine on feces instead (which may be gross, but at least is harmless). The Phi Song Nang are equally gross, but more dangerous. It is merely a head with entrails dangling from its neck, and it has a nasty tendency to use its long tongue to suck both feces and blood from people's bottoms.

Malaysia

Malaysia's Pennanggalan are a lot like Thailand's Phi Song Nang. The Pennanggalan, however, started out as an old and ugly woman. One day a passerby startled her so badly that she kicked herself under the chin, separating her head from her body. The head flew up into the treetops, a gory trail of intestines hanging from the stump of the neck. She might have been condemned to hang out in the tree for all eternity, but a helpful monster happened past and taught her the knack of stuffing her intestines back into her body and reattaching her head. She could then remove it again as the fancy took her. In her body-less form, she was prone to feasting on human flesh, and the unsuspecting traveler needed to be careful to search the treetops for her head with its dangling intestines. Even if he escaped being turned into her next meal, a drop of her blood falling down on him as he passed beneath her tree could make oozing sores appear on his skin, and he would likely die from a hideous disease. Like the Krassy of Thailand (and so many other blood-sucking creatures in the world) the Pennanggalan's preferred meal was newborn flesh. Her intestines would often become so bloated with the blood of her victims that she would have to soak them in a vat of vinegar to shrink them down enough to fit back inside her body. To protect their babies, Malaysians strung thorns around their windows and doors to snag her dangling intestines and trap her.

Another creature called the Langsuir was a beautiful woman in a flowing green robe that drifted through Malaysia's warm dark nights. Her black hair fell to her ankles, and her fingernails were as sharp as broken glass. After giving birth to a stillborn baby, the Langsuir had gone mad with grief. She escaped into the jungle, where as the years went by, she turned into a demon. She hunted and killed other women's babies and then pressed their bodies to the deep bloody hole at the back of her neck, so that their blood could flow into her. The Langsuir was so feared, the Malaysians

After the death of her own child, the Langsuir became insane with grief and emptiness.

began to suspect that a single demon could not be in as many places as she was rumored to be. A langsuir could also be created, they realized, if a woman died during childbirth. She would turn into an owl-woman, stealing fish from the fishermen when she could not get the human flesh she now craved. To prevent this terrible transformation, the long-ago Malaysians filled the dead woman's mouth with glass beads, put eggs in her armpits, and thrust needles into the palms of her hands. If they failed to do this and the woman became a langsuir, they would have to capture her, carefully following the proper procedures once they had her. Her nails and hair would need to be cut, and then the hair and clippings stuffed into the hole at the back of her neck. This would allow her to go back to her life, behaving like a normal woman, so long as the hole in her neck remained plugged.

India's Goddess of Destruction

Hinduism, one of the world's great religions, was born in India thousands of years ago. Its ancient scriptures (written down between 1100 and 1700 BCE from stories

Kali is often portrayed with her mouth wet and red with blood. Despite her terrifying appearance, many people in India worship her with great devotion, recognizing that Kali embodies both destruction and creation.

and wisdom that had been handed down orally for countless centuries before that) tell the tales of many gods and goddesses. The Goddess Kali is one of these. Bearing a skull-topped staff and clad in a tiger's skin, she wears a necklace of skulls around her neck. Like the Egyptian goddess Sekhmet, she is filled with a terrible and dangerous thirst for blood and destruction.

Kali's worshippers knew they must face her curse, the terror of death, as willingly as they accepted her blessings. For them, wisdom means learning that no coin has only one side: death cannot exist without life, and life cannot exist without death. By acknowledging this as it is embodied by Kali, many Hindus believe a state of peace can be reached even within life's chaos. Kali is clearly far more than any vampire, and despite her fearsome appearance, she is worshipped and loved in much of India. Her name means "The Black One," "Time," "Death," and "Beyond Time." She is the destroyer—but she is also the redeemer and creator. Out of destruction, she brings new life.

Kali puts flesh on our human fascination with death— as well as our race's most primitive belief that death is not the final end of life. Kali's place in the Hindu pantheon of gods acknowledges that life is full of change, that nothing lasts forever, that death cannot be escaped. At the same time, however, those who worship Kali rejoice in the knowledge that even death is full of creativity and the promise of new life.

chapter 4
AFRICA'S LIVING DEAD

Africa is a huge land, filled with many geographical regions and different groups of people. Across the deserts, savannahs, and jungles, stories of various terrifying creatures of death have been told and passed along through the centuries.

In parts of Ghana, Togo, and the Ivory Coast, for instance, the Asasabonsam are vampires with hooks for feet and iron teeth. Like terrible fishermen, they dangle their feet from trees to catch unwary passersby—and then they drain their bodies' blood. The Asasabonsam are also known to suck blood from the thumbs of sleeping people.

Meanwhile, the Ewe people in southeastern Ghana and southern Togo believed that a vampire spirit known as Adze possesses some sorcerers. This vampire looks like a firefly and flies around preying on young children, drinking their blood. If caught, it will revert to its human form.

In Surinam, the bat-woman known as the Axeman appears perfectly normal by day, but after dark, she flits through the village, seeking her prey. If she finds a sleeper whose foot is exposed, she carefully scrapes away a bit of flesh from the big toe until blood trickles out—and then she feeds until she is engorged. Her victim will wake up the next morning feeling drained and weak. A broom propped across the doorway, however, will usually keep an Axeman from entering.

In other regions of Africa, the Loango lay in its coffin with its eyes wide and staring. During life, he had been a sorcerer who communed with the other world, and now he was unable to close his eyes in death. Like his European brethren to the north, his strength waxed and waned with the moon—and he could also transform himself into a bat. Destroying a Loango requires that you burn him on a moonless night—or else nail him to the ground. If you burn him, be sure the fire consumes every tiny fragment of him, for even the smallest bit is enough for him to reshape himself. Be prepared for the terrible moans he will utter while he burns.

Along Africa's Gold Coast, the Ashanti people tell of the Obayifo, a witch or sorcerer whose spirit is able to leave the body and fly around at night like a glowing ball of light (a little like the Adze), feeding upon young

The Loango may be
unable to close their
eyes, even in death.

The vampire creatures of Africa, like their European cousins, sometimes took the form of a bat, but they were more likely to appear as a ball of mysterious light.

children. This vampire could blight crops as well as children, since it not only drank blood but was also partial to the juice of some fruits and vegetables. It could destroy entire fields of crops if it drank too much.

These creatures came to life in the minds of humans living far from Europe and Asia, and yet unmistakable similarities echo across the continents. And far to the south, in the Land Down Under, these same echoes can be heard.

chapter 5
AUSTRALIAN BLOOD SUCKERS

The island continent of Australia is separated from the rest of the world. Unique animals such as the platypus, the koala, and the kangaroo evolved there. No wonder then that Australian vampires and werewolves are different from anywhere else in the world. And yet, at the same time, they are frighteningly the same. . . .

The Aborigines of Australia tell of the Yara-Ma-Yha-Who, a four-foot-tall furry little red man with an enormous head and mouth. The creature has no teeth, so it swallows its food whole and uses octopus-like suckers on the ends of its toes and fingers to drain its victim of blood. Like some of the African and Asian blood-drinkers, it hides in trees and attacks people as they walk underneath. The Yara-Ma-Yha-Who swallows its

The Garkain has the bat-like appearance of the European vampire.

victims whole, sucks their blood, takes a nap—and then spits the person out. The process is not fatal, but if you are unlucky enough to be attacked more than once by this creature, you might gradually become shorter . . . and shorter . . . until eventually you become a Yara-Ma-Yha-Who yourself.

In Australia's northern territories, meanwhile, lives the Garkain, who is as big as a normal-sized man. He has bat-like wings, and a foul odor hovers around him in a cloud. If a hunter or lost child should stray into the Garkain's mangrove forest, he swoops from the trees, wrapping his wings around his victim. The unlucky person first chokes on the stench, and then slowly suffocates. The Garkain then consumes the person, first the blood, then the flesh. The victim's spirit will be condemned to wander the region, unable to find its way home to the final resting place of his people.

Aborigines also believed that each person had a second soul, which could sometimes wander off and

The Australian Werewolf

The Irrinja, the devil-dog, has the shape of a man but when a sandstorm comes, he lies down and lets the sand cover him. When the storm is over, at the cry of the butcher bird, the dune parts and the Irrinja emerges with a bristly muzzle, a hanging tongue, and enormous fangs. He will be thirsty for blood and hungry for flesh.

inhabit another person's body, especially after death. It might live in the bush for years, tormenting its living relatives, which was why dead bodies were weighted down or their legs were broken. These beings became vampire-like creatures of the night, sometimes known as Mrart. They were said to drag victims away from a campsite and consume them in the darkness.

The Talamaur was another kind of vampire found in Australia, as well as in other parts of Polynesia. This creature could communicate with the spirit world and used the spirits to do its bidding. It feasted on fresh corpses, draining them of their remaining life and blood. Basically, the Talamaur are the vultures of the vampire world, carrion eaters rather than predators.

10.

chapter 6
THE AMERICAS' BLOODY BEASTS

As people traveled across the oceans from Europe, Africa, and Asia to the Americas, they brought with them their folklore and legends. These stories mixed with those of the Native people already living in North and South America. The creatures that stepped out of these shared nightmares were a little different from the ones we have already described, but they were also the same old story: human beasts who were thirsty for blood.

West Indies

The African slaves who were brought to the West Indies carried with them the stories from their homeland, where they mixed with European folklore, to create a mixture of both. The Asema—sometimes also known as the Loogaroo—for example, was much like the Obay-ifo: by day she was an old lady, but by night, she shed her skin to become a flying, blood-drinking blue light. Her favorite site for bloodsucking was between a person's toes. If she didn't like the taste of the blood, she would move on—but if she liked it, she would drink her victim dry. Like some European vampires, she was both obsessive-compulsive and killed by sunlight when she was in her supernatural form—so if you scattered seeds or nails on the ground around your doors, they would keep her busy compulsively counting them until the sun rose, striking her dead. Another way to kill the Asema was to find her skin during the night when she was in her blue-light form, get it wet, and let it dry, so that it shrank. Then when she tried to squeeze back into her skin at the end of the night, she wouldn't be able to fit. The sun would find her still a blue light, and she would die.

Mexico

The land of Mexico mixed Native stories with those from Spain, to come up with its own potent mixture. The Cihuateteo is a Mexican vampire woman who started out life as either a stillborn baby or a mother who died in childbirth. Once transformed into this evil creature, however, it bites babies and paralyzes them

WHY IS THE SUN SO POWERFUL AGAINST VAMPIRES AND WEREWOLVES?

It makes sense if you think about it. Imagine that you've had a nightmare. You wake up in the dark, gripped by a paralyzing sense of fear, and huddle under your covers. As the first light of the new day creeps through your window, however, your fears gradually disappear. What seemed so terrifying in the dark now seems merely silly. The sunlight has killed the monsters.

while it feeds. The Cihuateteo flies, and its hands, arms, and face are as white as chalk. Filled with an unending hunger, it can be distracted from feasting on babies if you can fill it up with bread instead—and if you don't have any bread, say the stories, meteorites will do! Like so many vampire creatures, the Cihuateteo die if it is caught in sunlight.

The Tlahuelpuchi is another Mexican monster, a shape-shifting blood-drinker. As a young girl, she was cursed, and once she enter puberty and begins to menstruate, she begins to crave blood. At night, she transforms into an animal (a cat, a dog, a turkey, a vulture, or even a flea). Often, she leaves her human legs lying behind her in the shape of cross as she flees into the night in her animal form. Her favorite meal is—of course!—babies, but she will make do with the blood of adults or even cows. Her blood craving is connected to her menstrual cycle, so she only requires blood once a month. If you suspect someone of being a Tlahuelpuchi, offer her an enchilada with garlic in it. If she become sick after eating it, chances are good she's a blood-sucking monster.

Brazil

The Jararacas are nasty little were-snakes that feed from the breasts of nursing mothers. They push the human babies aside, and keep them quiet by stuffing the ends of their tales into the babies' mouths.

Another Brazilian creature, the Lobisomen, is a stumpy, little hunchback with bloodless lips, yellow skin, black teeth, and a bushy beard. Its bite turns women into nymphomaniacs (women who cannot get enough of sex). The only way to dispose of this little guy is

In the Americas, just as in Africa, in Asia, and in Europe, many shape shifters and blood drinkers were women, especially women who had died in childbirth or lost a baby. Childbirth was dangerous business in the days before modern medicine, and for many women it was a doorway to death.

to allow it to drink its fill of blood, which will make it drunk—and then impale it on a tree with a knife.

North American Native Tribes

The folklore of the Navajo tribe of the Southwestern United States tells of skinwalkers, humans that take the shape of animals, usually wolves. Skinwalkers must wear the actual skin of the animal into which they want to change. After transforming into a wolf or other animal, the skinwalker attacks, terrorizes, or kills people. It can read minds, which allows it to know exactly where its victims are at all times. Skinwalkers can be identified by their glowing red eyes when they are in their human forms.

To the north, the Algonquins of Eastern Canada tell of a being called the wendigo. When a person is lost and starving in the woods, usually during a harsh winter, he might turn into a cannibalistic monster called a wendigo. Other variations claim that a person can turn into a wendigo after being bitten by one, or even by dreaming about one. After transforming into a large beast, hunger and confusion drive the person to eat fellow tribe members, particularly naughty children. The only way to get rid of a wendigo is to kill it, and then burn the body.

In another part of North America, in the Southeast United States and Oklahoma, a group called the Seminole have their own monster myths. The stikini of the Seminole are also transformed humans, though in this lore, they change into owls. In order to transform, a person must vomit up her organs, leaving them in the woods. Stikini then prey on sleeping humans, drawing their hearts out of their mouths and devouring them. To change back into human form, they simply find the spot where they left their organs. However, if a hunter comes across the heap of bloody entrails in the woods, he can kill the stikini by destroying the organs.

The wendigo of the Algonquins was a human driven mad by hunger.

The Lure of Blood

We humans, wherever and whenever we live, seem to never get tired of hearing stories about blood. Whether it's the latest blood and gore on a forensic mystery like CSI—or the blood and darkness of the HBO series *True Blood*—or an ancient story of strange creatures that fly through the darkness, seeking their prey's blood—we are always fascinated. We may think these stories are disgusting or terrifying, but either way, we can't resist them.

Blood can mean purity—or guilt; birth—or death; destruction—or new life. It is the contradictory force that flows through our human identities. Like vampires and werewolves, we humans need blood to live.

And like vampires and werewolves, we can be evil and full of darkness and greed. In fact, in many ways, these monsters of the night are merely ourselves, a way to confront the cruelty in our own hearts. Like the Green Woman of Scotland, we can be both deadly and kind. Like her, we may appear beautiful, while all the while we hide our animal natures beneath our clothes. Like Russia's Wurdulac, we sometimes destroy the ones we love the most—and yet we are capable of self-sacrifice, of rising above our destructive tendencies. When our true natures are recognized and named, we too can be freed from our animal natures, just as the werewolves of Scandinavia were. Like so many vampire creatures, we humans are sometimes destructive to our children, sucking the life from the very ones to whom we gave life.

The blood that flows through us humans also drives us to find fresh possibilities and rise to new heights. Ultimately, blood is the symbol of our humanity, the common life that unites us around the world, despite our difference. We are all creatures of blood: we know we will die, and yet we hope we will live forever.

Blood symbolizes both our darkest forebodings about death and our hope that even in death we will find new life.

WORDS YOU MAY NOT KNOW

afflicted: Suffering from physical or mental harm.

carrion: Dead and rotting flesh.

compelled: Forced.

duality: Having to do with two things or types or things that, while seemingly opposites, are closely connected to each other.

exorcise: To get rid of an evil spirit, usually through a ceremony or ritual.

insidious: Harmful and evil, in a sneaky and tricky way.

memorializes: Serves as a reminder of.

pantheon: The group of gods from a certain mythology.

primitive: Having to do with early history or the early version of something.

reanimating: Bringing back to life.

sustains: Supports, keeping something going.

transformation: The change from one thing or state into another.

voracious: Eagerly craving and consuming large amounts of food.

Find Out More on the Internet

Encyclopedia Mythica
www.pantheon.org

Monstrous Werewolves
werewolves.monstrous.com/

Universal Vampire
vampires.monstrous.com/universal_vampire.htm

Vampires
www.vampires.com

Werewolves
www.werewolves.com

Further Reading

Dixon, J.M. *The Weiser Field Guide to Vampires: Legends, Practices, and Encounters Old and New.* San Francisco, Cal.: Red Wheel/Weiser, 2009.

Greer, John Michael. *Monsters: An Investigator's Guide to Magical Beings.* St. Paul, Minn.: Llewellyn Publications, 2001.

Peek, Philip M., and Kwesi Yankah. *African Folklore: An Encyclopedia.* New York: Routledge, 2009.

Smith, W. Ramsay. *Myths and Legends of the Australian Aborigines.* Mineola, N.Y.: Dover, 2003.

Summers, Montague. *The Vampire in Lore and Legend* (1928). Mineola, N.Y.: Dover, 2001.

Summers, Montague. *The Werewolf in Lore and Legend* (1933). Mineola, N.Y.: Dover, 2003.

Wright, Dudley. *Vampires and Vampirism: Legends from Around the World* (1914). Maple Shade, N.J.: Lethe Press, 2001.

Yumoto, Koichi, and Hiroyuki Kano. *Mythical Beasts of Japan: From Evil Creatures to Sacred Beings*. Tokyo, Japan: PIE Books, 2010.

Bibliography

Baring-Gould, Sabine. *The Book of Werewolves*, London, U.K.: Smith & Elder, 1865.

Belanger, Michelle. *Vampires in Their Own Words*. Woodbury, Minn.: Lewellyn Publications, 2006

Cooke, B. *Sacraments and Sacramentality*. New Haven, Conn.: Twenty-Third Publications, 1983.

Earhart, B. H. (ed.), *Religious Traditions of the World: A Journey through Africa, North America, Mesoamerica, Judaism, Christianity, Islam, Hinduism, Buddhism, China, and Japan*. New York: Harper-Collins, 1990.

Grahn, J. "Blood, Bread, and Roses: How Menstruation Created the World." bailiwick.lib.uiowa.edu/wstudies/grahn/chapt13.htm (12 June 2010).

Martos, Joann. *Doors to the Sacred: A Historical Introduction to Sacraments in the Catholic Church*. Liguori, Mo: Triumph, 2001.

Monstrous.com. www.monstrous.com (11 June 2010).

Ramsland, K. *The Science of Vampires*. New York: Berkley Boulevard, 2002.

Index

Asema 52
Aswang 33–34

bat 15, 42, 44, 48
blood-drinker 15, 54–55
blood-sucking 18, 20, 33, 36, 47, 49, 54
bloodthirsty 25, 27, 29
burn 21, 25, 30, 42, 56

Ch'iang Shih 31–32
Cihuateteo 52–54
coffin 19, 31, 42
corpse 3 29–30, 32–33, 49
curses 19, 23, 39, 54

demon 30–31, 36–37
devil 19–20, 49
Dracula 13, 15–16, 25

flesh 11, 13, 31–32, 36–37, 39, 42, 48–49, 60

garlic 27, 33, 54

Kali 38–39
Kasha 30–31
Krassy 35–36

Langsuir 36–37
Luderc 25, 27

nightmare 23, 27, 51, 53

Obayifo 42, 52

Pennanggalan 35–36
possess 30, 41

shape-shifting 17, 30, 54
skinwalker 55–56
sorcerer 19, 41–42
spirit 13, 15, 17, 21, 30, 34–35, 41–42, 48-49, 60
stikini 56

Transylvania 16, 25
trolls 24, 26

undead 19, 32
Upierczi 19

Wampir 20–21
wendigo 56–57
were-creatures 22, 26
witches 18–19, 21, 25, 42
Wurdulac 21, 58

Yara-Ma-Yha-Who 47–48

About the Author

The 1970s Gothic soap opera *Dark Shadows* had a formative influence on Adelaide Bennett when she was growing up. She continues to be interested in the darker side of the supernatural world, and enjoys reading and studying the history, psychology, and mythology that is interwoven with stories of the supernatural. With degrees in both psychology and writing, she enjoyed the opportunity to write about topics that combined her two fields of interest.

Picture Credits